TRINA

(Original Title: Trina's Boxcar)

by PATRICIA MILES MARTIN

Illustrated by Mac Conner

SCHOLASTIC BOOK SERVICES

NEW YORK • TORONTO • LONDON • AUCKLAND • SYDNEY • TOKYO

ISBN: 0-590-02579-1

Text Copyright © 1967 by Abingdon Press. Illustrations Copyright © 1968 by Scholastic Magazines, Inc. This edition is published by Scholastic Book Services, a division of Scholastic Magazines, Inc., by arrangement with Abingdon Press.

16 15 14 13 12 11   0 1 2 3/8
Printed in U.S.A.   11

To Barbara Sue Ameling

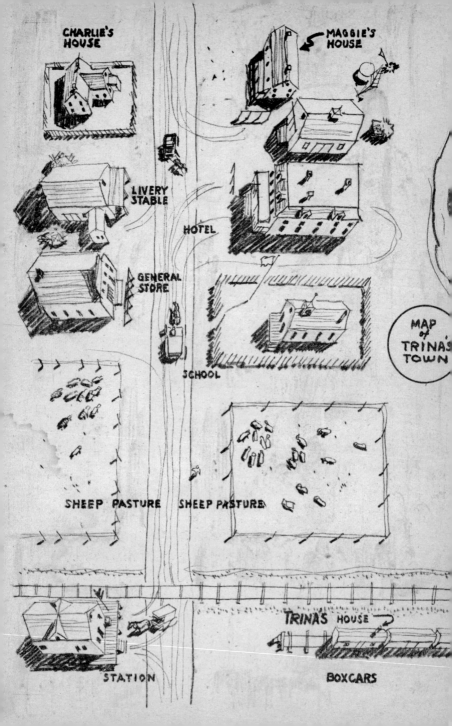

I

BESIDE THE BOXCAR where she lived, Trina wrote a name in the cinders with the heel of her shoe: M-A-G-G-I-E.

This was the name of the one girl Trina wanted for a friend — her first friend.

Trina couldn't remember a time when she had not lived in a boxcar set somewhere on a railroad siding near the depot. But the boxcar was never long in one town, and because they always moved on from town to town, it happened that Trina couldn't speak English. She could understand English and she could write it, but she couldn't speak it.

And so Trina had never had a friend. Not a real friend. Not one her own age to remember always.

Before, it hadn't really mattered much that she didn't know English. It certainly hadn't mattered at all here in this Wyoming town, for there had not been a girl her own age to talk to, either in the boxcars or in the houses on the hill.

But now, after this morning, it mattered.

It mattered very much.

It mattered because of this girl Maggie.

This morning the train coming from Denver had brought an important family to live in town. The three mothers from the Spanish-speaking families who lived in the boxcars on the siding stood together talking about it.

"The one getting off the train is the wife of the railroad superintendent," said Trina's mother, as she wrapped her hands in her orange-colored apron.

"Look," said Trina. "There's a girl — and she's *my* size, Mama."

The girl wore a brown coat. She had long braids.

"Red hair," said Trina's mother. "Beautiful."

Charlie Wilson and his father, who owned the

town stable, were at the station with a wagon. Their big black dog was sitting in the shade of the depot. Mr. Wilson had backed the wagon around close to the tracks, and its tail gate was down. Baggagemen slid a trunk out into the wagon.

Mr. Wilson helped the superintendent's wife up to the seat, but the girl and her father rode in back with Charlie.

The freight car carrying furniture and boxes was shunted over to a siding.

Trina ran up the hill behind the wagon. As she leaned into the wind, her purple dress clung to her knees. When she whirled and walked backward, her dress billowed out like washing on a line.

On each side of the road, on rolling hills that stretched beyond the fences, were the sheep — hundreds of sheep grazing together.

The wagon passed the hotel and went on to a large brown house. Trina stopped across the street to watch from a respectful distance.

The girl saw her and crossed over, swishing her skirt. She looked as though she wanted to laugh, and that made Trina want to laugh too. Oh, this could be a happy time with a girl her own size — a girl about her own age.

"My name's Maggie," the girl said. The wind blew her hair back from her forehead. "What's your name?"

"*Me llamo Trina.*" Trina was embarrassed that she had spoken in Spanish.

"Do you go to school?" Maggie smiled at Trina.

"*Sí,*" Trina answered.

Maggie waited for a moment and then moved backward.

Trina could have cried. When she needed the English words, where were they? She thought about this girl long after Maggie had skipped across the street.

Trina looked at the name she had written on the ground. Maggie had a smile and a dimple deep in each cheek and freckles — beautiful, beautiful freckles across her nose and under her blue eyes.

Trina noticed that one of her own shoelaces was dragging, and she reached down to make a neat bow. She pulled the loops tightly, and as she stooped there, her long black braids swung forward. Impatiently she pushed them back.

She hurried to the door of the boxcar. She needed to be understood. Mama and Jaime were speaking Spanish.

Her mother was sitting in a small rocking chair putting a patch on Jaime's pants. Jaime was waiting in his shirt.

A tear trickled down the side of Trina's nose.

"What happened?" her mother asked in Spanish.

"Mama, I went up the hill, and this Maggie—she talked to me. I couldn't think of the answer in English. I answered in Spanish, Mama."

"Crybaby," said Jaime in English.

"Remember to speak Spanish at home, please," Mama said.

"These are only wishing tears," Trina said.

"And what is it that you wish?" her mother asked.

"I want to learn to speak English more than anything in the world," Trina said. "Then I can have a friend when I go to school. The new girl. This Maggie."

"Perhaps this year you will learn," Mama said.

"But I think in Spanish, Mama, and the words come out in Spanish."

"Perhaps this year you will learn," Mama said, "because you will try very, very hard."

Jaime reached over and yanked at a ribbon on Trina's braid. "She's a dunce in school," he said.

"A terrible dunce. She was a dunce last year and a dunce the year before. She's still reading in the second reader. A big girl like Trina. She thinks the teacher should wait all day while she thinks of the answer."

"That is not so." Trina retied her ribbon. "I *know* the answer. It's just that I know it in Spanish. Nobody gives me time enough to think of the English words."

Jaime shrugged his shoulders. "All the same, I'm ashamed to have a dunce for a sister."

"Mama," Trina said, "did you hear what he said? I am *not* a dunce. In arithmetic I know the answers, because we do them with chalk on the blackboard. In spelling we write the words on paper, and I know them all. Well, almost all. It is only in reading out loud."

"Why can't you be quick like me?" Jaime asked pleasantly.

"Enough," said their mother. "Stop teasing her, Jaime. You have gone to school a year longer than Trina. You are a year older. In another year she may catch up with you."

"But I can't wait a year," Trina said. "I have to know *now*."

"Take it little by little," Mama said. "Perhaps when the new teacher comes, perhaps when school starts again, she will understand. Perhaps she will give you time to answer. And until then remember that the way to have a friend is to be one."

Trina left Jaime waiting for Mama to finish the patch on his pants and went outside.

She wiped her eyes on her petticoat and brushed her skirts back into place.

She thought about Mama's words. The way to have a friend is to be one. How could this be done without English? How?

2

TRINA STOOD GAZING up the hill at the town.

Looking from the tracks were many things to see. There were sheepherders' dogs trotting behind sheepherders' wagons. And sometimes six horses pulled a wagon loaded high with bales of hay, or a grunting pig got away and rooted around the railroad station until its owner found it and took it away. And always there were the sheep that grazed on the hillsides.

Trina could remember many towns.

Some were much like this Wyoming town, with the main road leading from the boxcars and reaching across the railroad tracks and straight up the sagebrush-covered hill to a cluster of small brown buildings.

These buildings were the town.

On one side of the wide dirt street were small square stores. From the railroad tracks these looked like wooden boxes set out in a row. But on the other side of the street, the very big, two-story hotel with a covered porch around two sides looked like a castle. And beyond the castle was Maggie's father's house.

Trina thought of her own strong father. Every time they were just beginning to belong in the town where they lived, the superintendent sent Papa somewhere else. Then an engine came and hooked onto their boxcar and pulled it to another town.

"*Este es mi pueblo,*" Trina said to herself, "*y yo quiero quedarme aquí.*" Trina sighed. Slowly and carefully she repeated the thought in English:

"This is *my* town and I want to stay here."

Inside her boxcar the bunks for sleeping were curtained off with turkey-red calico. The rest of the car was for cooking and eating, washing and ironing.

The chimney from the little black stove went straight up and then curved to go out through the side wall of the car. Their floor was covered with linoleum, scrolled with red roses in brown and green wreaths. On the wall opposite the wide door was a chest that held the treasures that Mama had brought with her from Mexico.

An amber-colored kerosene lamp with a clear, shining glass chimney stood in the middle of a plain pine table.

Trina and Jaime loved the freedom of the boxcar. They were in and out of it all day long, tracking in dirt in the summertime and snow in the winter. A whisk of a broom, and the car was clean. A piece of coal in the little black stove, and it was snug and warm. And the bright yellow pottery pitcher filled with wild iris made everything as cheerful as sunshine.

Every morning and every night the passenger trains passed by as they came huffing through the town, stopping only long enough to let a sheep rancher swing down to the platform, or to take a passenger aboard.

Freight trains, too, clanked by all day, and sometimes into the night. Trina loved the deep thunder of their passing.

Two other families lived there on the siding. All these mothers and fathers kept to themselves and spoke only Spanish together, so their children would not forget the language of their fathers and *their* fathers before them.

Trina thought it was all very well not to forget Spanish, but it was inconvenient not to speak English. She needed desperately to know how to speak English now.

Ricardo and Pablo lived in the boxcar next to them, and Flavio Valdez in the one beyond. Counting Jaime, four boys lived on the tracks, with no girl except Trina among them. And there was no place for Trina in their games.

"Who wants to play baseball with a girl?" Ricardo said.

"Or even marbles," said Pablo.

"Go help Mama," Jaime always said.

All the girls up on the hill were much older than Trina. Often they stopped to speak to her. Trina understood everything they said, but she could never think of the English words quickly enough to answer. The girls would smile and walk on.

Across the street from the hotel horses and buggies were lined up along the hitching rack in front of the general store. There was not a sign of the new girl.

Trina crossed the tracks and stopped at the pasture fence. A ewe[1] trailed behind a small flock of sheep, and it stopped and lifted its head and stood so still that it looked like a statue carved from gray stone.

Trina pulled up a handful of wild grass and called softly, *"Estás tan linda."*

The ewe limped toward her. It accepted the grass and chewed solemnly. Trina liked the way the ewe looked at her, trusting, unafraid. She reached through the fence and twisted her fingers in its soft fleece.

"You are beautiful. Underneath the top of your wool, you are yellow, beautiful." She felt like laughing. "And to you it doesn't matter that I speak in Spanish. You understand."

Trina gathered handful after handful of grass, and the ewe followed along beside her on the other side of the fence. When it finally turned away, Trina slowly walked to the top of the hill.

She stood across the street in front of Maggie's house. And then she saw Charlie Wilson and Maggie coming from the store, running along the street toward Maggie's house.

Trina waited, hoping they would turn back and ask her to follow them.

[1] a female sheep

3

AT MAGGIE'S HOUSE, her mother opened the door wide. She did not look across the street where Trina watched and waited. Maggie and Charlie went inside.

Trina stood there alone. Then she started downhill, running, leaning back to keep her balance.

When she reached home, the boxcar smelled of ironing and hot blue gingham.

"I'll help you, Mama," Trina said.

"Good," Mama answered. "You can iron the flat pieces. You do them very well."

Trina shook out a towel and laid it across the board propped between chair back and table. She pushed the iron forward and pulled it back — forward and back — forward and back. Perhaps things would be different when school started again.

Until school started there was really nothing to do except to help Mama in the boxcar and wait for vacation to be over.

She thought about going to school, and she knew that she felt two ways about it.

"I want to go and I don't want to go," she said to her mother. Even so, she counted the days, marking them off on the calendar that hung by the door. Seven days to go, on the September page, before school started.

Six days later Charlie Wilson came to the boxcar.

"Teacher's coming this morning. Mr. Marshall is hitching up to meet her. She's going to live at the hotel. Her name's Miss Grace, and she's coming from Denver."

Trina washed her face and brushed her hair and smoothed her purple dress with the palms of her hands.

"How do I look?" she asked.

"Beautiful," her mother answered. "None more beautiful than you."

"Terrible," Jaime said. "Hair straight like a horse's tail." He pulled a braid. "And she's skinny."

"Mama, I did not ask him," Trina said.

"Let her alone, Jaime," Mama said.

Sixteen boys and girls and Mr. Marshall from the hotel were at the railroad station when the train came rumbling down the track.

Trina stood back from the crowd, waiting and watching. The train stopped, and there she was — the new teacher. She was smiling and she was young, and her hair was as black as Trina's.

"Welcome to town," Mr. Marshall said. "We hope you're going to like it here."

The teacher looked at Jaime and Charlie, who had pushed to the front. "I like it already," she said.

Mr. Marshall helped her into the buggy, and all the boys began shoving one another. Ricardo turned a handspring.

Thoughtfully Trina walked back to the boxcar. "This teacher will understand," she thought. "Tomorrow I will tell her that I speak slowly in English." She threw her arms around her mother's waist.

"Mama, how will I find the English words tomorrow to ask the teacher if she will wait for me? How?"

"Practice them," Mama said. "Think of the words over and over."

Now was the time to ask Mama an important question. "Mama, if you'd let Papa and Jaime speak English at home, maybe I'd learn, Mama. We'd both learn. You and I. Papa and Jaime speak English all the time when they're not in the boxcar. Why can't we listen and learn at home, Mama?"

Mama put her hand on Trina's shoulder.

"We will continue to speak Spanish at home. At school you will learn English — little by little."

The next morning Trina was practicing the English words in her mind. "I speak slowly. I speak slowly."

She tugged on her heavy black stockings and pulled them straight. She pulled her shoelaces tight and tied neat bows. She brushed her hair over and over, and fastened the ribbons that held the braids. She lifted her dress from its nail and slipped it carefully over her head.

Then she smoothed the gray blankets on the

bunks and went to help Mama set the table for breakfast.

"Teacher has a gold watch," Jaime said between noisy bites of toast.

"And she smiles," Trina said. "This is more important than having a watch."

"Oh, I don't know," Jaime said. "With a watch she'll know when it's time for recess."

After breakfast Mama handed Papa a lunch box. "Time to go. Papa to work, and Jaime and Trina to school."

Trina hurried alongside the tracks until she came to the path that led to the schoolhouse. Then she walked slowly with her back very straight. She carried the reader that she had studied last year. Only the second reader. But today the teacher would take this one and give her the third. That would be a little bit better — that would be much better. Trina smiled to herself.

Some of the boys and girls were already in the schoolyard. Maggie and two of the older girls were sitting on the steps. Flavio and Charlie Wilson were scuffling and pushing Abner Marshall.

Trina walked past Flavio and Charlie, past Abner. Maggie looked up and smiled and Trina smiled back.

"*Buenos días,*" Trina said. There it was. Spanish again. She felt her face grow hot. "I can't even remember an easy little thing like 'good morning,'" she thought. "It comes out in Spanish, as quickly as I think it." She stepped inside the schoolroom door and waited quietly.

The teacher was sitting at her desk. She wore a dress the color of the blue in the American flag. She looked up at Trina and smiled.

Now was the time — now was the time for Trina to speak.

4

"Good morning. Will you have a desk here?" The teacher pointed with her pen, and Trina walked forward and sat down.

She laid the reader on her desk. Reaching for one of her braids, she untied and retied the red bow. Perhaps now — no, *muy tarde*.

The teacher had looked at her watch and tapped the bell on her desk. Boys and girls trooped in noisily from the schoolyard, and the teacher opened a little black book.

Trina knew that now all their names would be written in the book. This would be a quiet time.

No one would speak except to answer the teacher.

"I'm glad to see you today," the teacher said. "I know that we'll have a happy year. I'm Miss Grace. Please answer the questions I'm going to ask."

She started with Maggie. The teacher's pen scratched in her little book as she went from one to the other — Maggie Tolley, Charlie Wilson, his big sister Elizabeth, Abner Marshall, and all the rest.

Finally it was Trina's turn.

"And what is your name?" The teacher was smiling encouragingly.

Trina drew a deep breath and before she could answer, Jaime was talking. He talked loud and fast.

"Her name's Trinidad Gonzales. That's because we've got an uncle who lives in Trinidad, Colorado. You can call her Trina. We all do. She can't speak English. She can do spelling and writing and arithmetic, but she's only reading in the second-grade book. My name's Jaime Gonzales."

The teacher laughed. "Thank you. I'll get back to you in a few minutes, Jaime." She went to the next desk — past Trina.

Trina felt like crying. But she held her head high and blinked hard to keep the tears away.

This would be like last year. *Nadie le esperaría.* No one would wait for her.

When the names were all in the book, the teacher opened her desk and stacked the readers in a row. She looked in her book and started to call the names for reading.

"Trina. May I have your reader?" She turned it over in her hands. "You will be ready for the third." The teacher handed Trina a third reader. "Let me hear you read the first lesson, please."

Trina stood in the aisle beside her desk and Miss Grace waited. Trina looked at the page. The words were jumbled together. She didn't see one that she remembered.

The teacher reached for another book. "Suppose you try this one?"

Trina was hot with shame. This second reader now in her hands she knew by heart. But something had happened. She couldn't breathe. She couldn't see for the tears. She couldn't think.

Then the teacher was reaching for the first reader. Trina backed away to the door. Once outside, she turned and ran like the wind.

5

SHE RAN LIKE THE WIND, down the path, on to her own boxcar. She pushed back the red curtains and threw herself down on the bunk.

"What is the matter?" her mother asked.

Trina couldn't tell her. She couldn't speak for crying. She cried until she couldn't cry any longer. Mama smoothed her shoulder and waited.

Finally Trina sat up and showed the book to her mother.

"The teacher didn't wait. The teacher laughed at me when Jaime told my name. This is a first reader. I am not going back to school."

That night at supper, they all sat around the table — Mama, Papa, Jaime, and Trina.

Mama poured hot chocolate into mugs for Trina and Jaime.

"I am sorry to hear that you are not going to school any more," her father said. "How else will you learn?"

"I will learn at home," Trina said. "Someone will help me."

"Jaime will help," Mama said.

"I don't want Jaime," Trina said. She looked at her father. "You, Papa, you shall help me. Every night after work you can listen while I read."

"And why not?" asked her father.

"Why *not?*" Mama was excited. "You ask why *not?* Because the book she must read is printed in English and not in Spanish. You speak English, Papa, but you cannot read it."

"Of course I speak English," Papa said. "How else would I understand when the foreman asks that a rail be replaced?"

"To you the English words would be like the scratches of the hen," Mama said.

"I do not plan to read, Mama. I will only listen. And when I listen, who shall know whether I listen in English or in Spanish." He tapped Mama's shoulder with a forefinger. "Listening will be easy for me. You will see. I will listen. Every night Trina shall read and I will listen."

"I have only the first reader," Trina said.

"Perhaps that is best," said Papa. "We begin at the bottom. We start for the top."

He held the book open on his knee.

As Trina read, Papa listened. He waited patiently. She read slowly, and he did not hurry her. Not once.

At the end of one week she had read through the first reader.

"How do I sound, Papa?" she asked.

"Magnificent," said Papa. "Jaime will take this back to school and ask for a second reader when he goes to school tomorrow. We are ready for number two."

The next day Jaime promised to bring back number two, and Trina watched as he swaggered off down the tracks. She could see Charlie Wilson waiting for him by the path ahead. *Friends* — Trina thought. How does one be a friend when she can't talk?

That afternoon she went up the hill to the store and practiced reciting in English the things her mother wanted. Trina had written the list in English. Then if something happened and she forgot again, she could offer the written list to Mr. Green.

"Sugar — ten cents' worth, please; one dozen eggs — brown eggs, please; beans — fifteen cents; white thread for buttons, please."

She hoped to remember.

When she walked into the store, Mr. Green was wrapping a package for Maggie's mother. He slid it across the counter. "Anything else, Mrs. Tolley?"

"No, thank you. I think this is all." Then she saw Trina.

"Shouldn't you be in school today?" Mrs. Tolley asked.

Trina nodded. Mrs. Tolley looked worried.

"Is someone ill at your house?" Mrs. Tolley asked.

Trina shook her head. Luckily for her, Mr. Marshall came into the store and spoke to Mrs. Tolley.

Trina went to the counter. She held the paper crumpled in her hand. "Sugar — ten cents' worth, please."

Mr. Green reached for a big scoop and measured

the sugar on his scales. He emptied it into a paper sack and twisted the top. "There you are."

"One dozen brown eggs, please."

Mr. Green counted the eggs. "Two, four, six, eight, ten, twelve. You'll have to be careful of this sack, Trina."

"Beans — fifteen cents," Trina said. "White thread for buttons."

Mr. Green opened a little thread case and chose a spool of coarse thread. He wrapped it in a wisp of paper. "I see you aren't in school today, Trina."

Trina looked at a little black spot on the counter and waited.

When Mr. Green weighed the beans, she picked up her packages and hurried outside before Mr. Green mentioned anything more about school.

Trina felt like hiding. She hurried on, past the barn where Mr. Wilson kept his young bull, past the hotel where a one-horned goat grazed by the path, on down the hill, past the sheep that fed beyond the road.

She heard voices, boys' voices. School was over for the day. Jaime was shouting louder than the others as he came wobbling down the road on Charlie Wilson's bicycle.

Charlie Wilson was running along beside him. Jaime put out a foot and steadied himself.

"¿*A dónde vas?*" Trina asked.

"She wants to know where we're going," Jaime explained to Charlie. He turned back to Trina. "We're going to the bottom of the hill. How do I look on a bicycle?"

"*Bien,*" said Trina. "*Y tu debiera llevar los paquetes. Estás andando a bicicleta.*"

Jaime translated for Charlie. "She thinks I ought to carry the packages. She said that I'm riding." He turned to Trina. "I can't. I need two hands on the handlebars."

"Sure you can," Charlie said. "You can steer with one hand. Nothing to it."

Trina handed the packages over to Jaime and watched his progress down the road. Charlie was galloping along to keep up with him, and his black dog was following close behind.

Jaime and Charlie were good friends. Everyone needed a good friend to make things fun, Trina thought.

She watched Jaime start down the hill.

In the distance pines leaned beside a twisted fence along the crest of the hill, and nearby a sparrow sat on a fence post and chirped cheerfully.

Over by the station was a big box, and Trina
wondered what was in it. She crossed through the
pasture, walking slowly.

The ewe bleated softly and came to her. Trina
stopped and lovingly put her fingers deep in the
lamb's wool. The ewe went with her to the fence.
Trina crawled under the barbed wire and went on
to the railroad station.

The side of the box next to the building was open.
Trina peeked in. It was empty. She pulled and
tugged and squeezed inside, hiding there.

The box had the good smell of new lumber. She
thought about Mr. Green and Mrs. Tolley and Mr.

Marshall, and most of all she thought about Maggie. This town was Trina's town, *her* own town, and she liked the people in it. She even liked Charlie Wilson and Abner Marshall. Perhaps she could tell them so in English. Mama had said that the way to have a friend was to be one. But you couldn't go right up to someone and say "I like you" in English. Or could you? You'd be too shy, maybe. But those English words would be easy to remember.

She practiced. "I like you. I like you."

Then she heard heavy footsteps.

"Who's mumbling in this box?" a voice said.

6

I⊤ WAS THE STATIONMASTER. He tipped the box and swung it away from the building. "Well, well, well. It's Trina. How was school today, Trina?"

Trina couldn't explain. Too many words were needed for this. She decided that her own boxcar was probably the best place for hiding. At least there no one would ask her any embarrassing questions.

Outside her boxcar she heard loud voices.

Inside, Jaime and Mama were shouting at each other angrily.

"It's Trina's fault," Jaime was saying. "It's Trina's fault."

Trina peeked inside.

Jaime was standing in the middle of the boxcar and Mama had her hands on her hips. Broken eggs were mashed against his pants and shirt. Bits of eggs and eggshell were caught in his black hair. "It's her fault, Mama. I fell off Charlie's bicycle. It's her fault. Maybe she doesn't know English. But she knows Spanish. She should have told me there were eggs in the sack."

"Trina will come in and start picking off eggshells," Mama said. "Call her. Oh there you are, Trina. Begin at once. When there is trouble in this family, each one helps."

And even when there was no trouble, Trina helped in the boxcar. She dusted the furniture and swept the floor. She helped with the cooking and the ironing, and gathered wild flowers for the yellow pitcher on the table.

"Each day the teacher calls your name and no one answers," Jaime said late one afternoon. "Each day the teacher asks why you are not in school and I say nothing."

"And how does it happen that you say nothing?" Trina asked. "Always, when I am there, you speak for me. You don't wait to let me talk. You say something. Anything. You say, 'Trina can't read.' "

She started after him and he retreated, yelling loudly, "Mama, Trina's starting a fight. Mama!"

"This is enough," Mama said. "Let me hear no more."

Trina ran outside so Mama would not see that she was crying.

Outside she stopped and wiped her eyes. She looked up the hill toward Maggie's house.

Some of the boys were playing ball across the street from the hotel, and on the hotel veranda two men sat on a bench feeding the goat.

Trina recognized Mr. Green's horse and buggy standing near the tracks. Mr. Green must have stopped there to watch the train go by. The reins were slack, and old Ruby grazed beside the fence. The buggy was turned toward the pasture.

As Trina started off toward the depot, the horse ambled a little way and stopped to reach down for a clump of grass. The wheels of the buggy now rested on the tracks. Something was wrong.

Trina ran toward the buggy calling, "*Señor Green. Señor Green.*"

When she reached the buggy, it was empty. Far

away the train whistle blew. Trina ran to old Ruby's head and pulled at the bridle.

"*Ruby*," Trina said. "*¡Anda, anda!*"

The whistle was louder. Ruby snorted ill-naturedly and jerked her head out of reach. The horse — this Ruby — didn't understand Spanish. "Gitty up — gitty up," Trina shouted in English.

There was shouting from the hotel, and Trina's mother called from the boxcar. Ruby lowered her head again, and Trina grabbed the bridle and tugged. "*Ven, ven* — come on, Ruby. *¡Ahora!* At once."

Trina could hear the rumble of the train and the frantic whistle.

7

THE HORSE AMBLED FORWARD. The wheels caught against the tracks, and they thumped across, rocking the buggy from side to side. Ruby and buggy were safe over the tracks.

The train came hissing, wheels sliding. It stopped in front of the station. The conductor and the brakeman ran back alongside the train.

Trina's mother had come from the boxcar and boys were coming from every direction.

"What's going on here?" the conductor asked. "Don't you know you could have caused a train

wreck with that horse on the track? And the horse would have been killed too. Who let you bring that horse down here?"

Trina couldn't answer — not even in Spanish.

Men came running down the hill.

"She didn't bring the buggy here," someone said. "That's Green's horse."

"That's my horse," Mr. Green said. He could hardly talk. "I left her standing in front of the store."

"That little black-haired girl got the horse off the tracks," a man said.

The conductor shoved his cap toward the back of his head. "Whew. I haven't had such a scare in years. I thought we'd hit that horse." He patted Trina's shoulder. "You're a very smart little girl."

When the train pulled out, the engineer blew his whistle. Trina knew that he blew it just for her.

"Bring your mother and come with me," Mr. Green said. He helped her mother into the buggy, and Trina climbed up beside her. Mr. Green talked all the way up the hill.

"When I looked out and saw that Ruby was gone, I thought at first she'd only wandered off a few steps; and then when I saw where she was, I started running. When that train whistle blew, I knew I didn't have a chance. Then I saw Trina."

Boys and girls were running along beside the buggy, laughing and shoving each other. The teacher came hurrying from the hotel.

Quite a crowd gathered while Mr. Green tied Ruby to the hitching rail. "I'll never trust her again," he said. "She gets tied after this."

Inside the store he led Trina to a glass counter. "Here's something intended for a girl like you," he said.

Behind the glass were two beautiful dolls. "They came yesterday. You may have whichever you want. You choose."

Trina looked at the dolls. One had shining black hair and the other had hair the color of gold.

"I know which you'll choose," Mr. Green said. "Look at that one. Black hair. Big brown eyes. Looks like you."

Trina shook her head.

Back of the case Mr. Green slid aside a wooden panel and took out the second doll. "Are you sure this is the one you want?"

The doll had eyes as blue as lupine. Trina lowered its head and its eyelids closed. It had real eyelashes.

"*Me gusta,*" she said. "I like it."

"It's yours," Mr. Green said.

"I wish I'd been there when old Ruby stopped on the tracks," Jaime said.

Flavio Valdez pushed him. "What would *you* have done with a doll!"

The two boys locked arms in quick good-natured scuffling.

"Trina's lucky," Ricardo said.

"Our town's lucky," Mr. Green corrected him. "Trina's not the lucky one. The town's lucky to have a girl as brave as Trina growing up in it."

"Trina spoke English to old Ruby when the train was coming," Flavio said. "Did you know, Trina? I heard you."

Trina shook her head.

Then the teacher had an arm around Trina's shoulder and was giving her a hug. "I need to have you back at school," the teacher said. "We all need you."

Trina tried to speak. One of these days soon all the English words that she needed would come, and when they did, Trina would talk a lot, for she had so much to say.

The teacher was still smiling. "Perhaps I didn't give you time enough to answer? Perhaps I didn't wait long enough? Will you come back to school tomorrow and give me another chance? Please?"

Trina nodded. Never had she been happier. *Never — so happy. Nunca tan felíz.* Her thoughts were a jumble of Spanish and English.

On the way home her mother wanted to know what had been said.

When Trina told her, her mother looked pleased. "Every day when Papa comes home from work, he and Jaime will speak English at home," she said. "And you and I will try to speak also. We will listen and learn. I must understand when words like these are spoken to my children."

When Papa got home that night, there was much to tell him. Everyone was talking at once. Papa heard about the doll in Spanish and in English.

"It is beautiful," he said. "But I, myself, prefer black hair and big brown eyes like yours, Trina."

Trina sat in the rocking chair. "I have named her

Ana Maria," she said. The doll wore a blue dress trimmed with lace at the neck and a petticoat with lace all the way around the hem. "See," she said to her mother. "There is even lace on the pants."

Jaime sat at the table drawing pictures with colored crayons. He looked at her slyly.

Este Jaime. One could never guess what he was thinking.

As she rocked, she tipped the doll backward and the eyelids closed. "She is asleep," Trina said.

"Good," Mama said. "Since she sleeps, put her to bed and go to Mrs. Valdez and borrow a cup of sugar. Brown sugar."

"Why can't Jaime go?"

"Many good things have happened to you today, so perhaps it would be nice to let Jaime enjoy his drawings."

Trina pushed aside the red curtains. She laid Ana Maria on the gray blanket with her head on a pillow. "*Descansa. Vuelvo pronto.*"

On the way to the Valdez boxcar she saw a pig lazily coming toward her.

"*Vete,*" Trina said. The pig came closer.

"*No tengo tiempo para cerdos hoy día.*" Still it did not leave. Even the pig did not understand

Spanish. "Go away. I do not have time for pigs today." Trina flapped her skirt at him. And that the pig understood. But she did not like the way he looked at her — unfriendly, suspicious.

She watched while Mrs. Valdez measured out the sugar and packed it well into the cup. Carefully, in order not to spill so much as one brown crystal, Trina carried it back home.

She helped her mother prepare supper. She stirred the pot of beans that bubbled on the stove.

Outside, Jaime and Flavio were playing and shouting.

"Shall I call Jaime?" Trina asked.

"Please," her mother answered.

Trina called from the doorway. "Jaime. Mama says to come for supper."

She went toward the bunk. "And I will allow Ana Maria to sit beside me at the table."

"Mama, Papa," she called. "*¡Mira, ve que ha pasado!*"

8

TRINA WAS CRYING LOUDLY. She stood beside the bunk.

Jaime slid into his place at the table. His straight black hair fell over his eyes, and he looked in his plate.

"What has happened?" asked their father.

Jaime answered. "The doll has chicken pox."

"He did it, Papa. He did it with his crayons."

"Now, now," Papa said. "To cry at mealtime is bad. Not only for the one who cries, but for all."

"Let me look." Mama inspected the doll and reached for a cloth. She rubbed carefully. "No damage is done. The spots will come off, every one. After supper Jaime will take off what he has put on."

"No, Mama. I don't want him to touch my doll. *I* will take the spots off." She looked at Jaime and did not like the way he looked — secretly laughing, full of tricks so no one could know what to expect.

After supper she felt kinder toward Jaime.

She laid Ana Maria on the bunk. "I will allow her to have chicken pox until morning," she said. She got her reader. "You will still help me, Papa, even though I have promised to go back to school?"

"Certainly," Papa said.

Trina went back to school, and every night Papa held the reader and listened while she read.

Mama listened too. Trina spoke words and more words, but she was still shy and unsure of herself with Maggie and the older girls.

In school she read through the first reader and part of the way through the second. She read slowly, but she read well.

One Friday after school Maggie spoke to Jaime

and Trina. "Tomorrow's my birthday, and I'm having a party. I'd like it if you and Trina would come."

Jaime kicked a pebble from the path.

"It will be at two o'clock tomorrow," Maggie said. "Charlie Wilson is coming, and Flavio, and Abner Marshall, and all the others."

Trina looked at Maggie. Friendship. She would be a friend to Maggie. She swallowed hard and spoke in English. "I like you."

Everyone laughed except Trina. She felt hot with her embarrassment. She could hardly believe that Maggie was laughing at her.

"No voy a tu fiesta," Trina said.

"She says she won't come to your party," Jaime said. He shrugged his shoulders. "I guess she doesn't want to go. I'll go, I guess."

Trina told her mother what had happened.

How wonderful it was to tell her troubles to Mama in Spanish. How wonderful to speak Spanish together. It was a beautiful, beautiful language. At the moment Trina didn't care if she *ever* spoke English.

"Well," Mama said, "even though they laughed, this should not make you cry. They are at fault. Not you. Sometimes boys and girls do not know how to accept a compliment with grace. Perhaps until they learn this, you will show that you like people rather than tell them."

"But I do not like Maggie now," Trina said. "Perhaps I hate her. I am not quite sure."

"You will never have friends if you expect them to be without fault," Mama said.

That evening their mother ironed a white shirt

for Jaime. She reached for a white dress and laid it over the ironing board.

"I am not going to the party, Mama," Trina said.

"You have not yet forgiven Maggie?" her mother asked.

"No, Mama."

"Very well. You need not go, of course. However, I will iron the dress, for you may feel differently tomorrow. You will take presents when you go."

"What presents?" Trina asked.

Their mother set the iron on the stove. "Let me think." She lifted the lid of the little chest at the side of the car. "Perhaps we might make a doll's dress. Maggie will have a doll like yours on her birthday. Flavio's mother was in the store when her father bought it. The doll in the glass counter."

She shook out a short length of red material sprigged with tiny yellow flowers. "See. I saved this to make an apron. Instead of making the apron, we will measure your Ana Maria and we will make a dress for Maggie's new doll. We will start at once."

"But if I do not go to the party?"

"You could then have a beautiful dress that will

fit your Ana Maria. This is for you alone to decide."

"I'm not going to give a doll's dress," Jaime said.

He reached on the shelf for a baking-powder can that held coins he had saved. He twisted off the top and emptied the coins on the table. He brushed half of them into the palm of his left hand and slid them into his pocket. "I'll buy a present for Maggie. I'll stop at the store and get something on the way to the party." He put the rest of the coins back in the can and twisted the top tightly shut.

"What will you buy?" Trina asked.

"A surprise," said Jaime.

Mama and Trina measured and cut and sewed to make a dress to fit a doll.

The next afternoon Jaime dressed for the party.

Trina looked at her white dress, crisp with Mama's starch. It would be beautiful with her red sash. She remembered Maggie's laughter. "I can't go," she said to her mother.

"Very well," Mama said. "And the present for Maggie. Do you choose to give this?"

"Yes. I choose to give it. I will send it by Jaime," Trina said.

She watched the boys and girls going up the hill to Maggie's house.

That afternoon she helped with ironing and sweeping and dusting. In the middle of the afternoon Mama made hot chocolate and they each had a sweet roll with it. Even so, the time dragged until Jaime came home. The afternoon was so long.

"But I am not sorry I stayed home, Mama. I couldn't have gone."

"I understand," Mama said.

When Jaime came home, he took off his white shirt and his Sunday trousers and put on his jeans and his blue and white checked shirt.

"Everything happened at that party," Jaime said. "It was fun. Mrs. Tolley dropped the birthday cake, and if it hadn't been for me, Maggie wouldn't have had any candles to blow out."

"What do you mean?" Mama asked.

"Well, when Mrs. Tolley dropped the cake, I picked up the candles and put them on my present," Jaime said.

"What was your present?" Trina asked.

"Gumdrops," said Jaime. "I put a candle on each gumdrop. It was as good as a cake. Mrs. Tolley lighted them, and Maggie made a wish and blew them out."

"What did Maggie wish?" Trina asked.

"How could I know?" Jaime asked. "When you blow out candles and make a wish, you don't tell what it is."

"And the doll's dress?" Trina asked. "What did Maggie say when she saw it?"

"I don't remember," Jaime said.

9

The next day at school Maggie walked straight to Trina.

"Trina. Thank you for the doll's dress. It's the prettiest dress I ever saw. It fits my doll." She pushed her red braids over her shoulders, and the dimples came in her cheeks. *"Trina. Me gusta,"* she said.

Everybody laughed, even Trina. Maggie too.

"I sound funny," Maggie said. "Spanish words are hard. But if you want to, I can try to speak Spanish while you try to speak English."

"You sound funny, Maggie," Jaime said.

"I know. Everybody does at first," Maggie said. "Now I will say 'thank you' to Trina, and Trina can say 'you're welcome' in English. Now listen, Trina. Say it after me: 'You are welcome.'"

Trina repeated the words slowly: "*Say it after me, you are welcome.*"

Maggie bent over with laughter.

Trina felt her own face crinkling. She blinked to keep back the tears.

"Don't pay any attention to her," Jaime said. "She cries easy. She cries no matter what happens."

"*Ríense,*" Trina said. "*No me importa.*"

"She says she doesn't care if you laugh," Jaime said. "She cares. She's crying."

"Oh well," Maggie said. "It's not fun to play with her anyway. If I laugh, she cries. And she won't even *try* to speak English."

Trina didn't stay to watch Maggie go up the hill. She went behind the boxcar and kicked the dirt until the air was thick with yellow-red dust.

"Why you are so dirty?" Mama asked pleasantly in English.

"You have it backward, Mama," Trina said in Spanish. "It should be 'Why are you so dirty?'"

"Good," said Mama. "One of us is learning English."

Trina helped Mama in the boxcar and thought about Maggie. If she wanted Maggie to be a friend, she would have to do more than learn English. She would have to be a friend. She would have to laugh with Maggie.

She laughed out loud.

"Why do you laugh?" Mama asked.

"I am practicing," Trina said.

And suddenly she and Mama laughed together.

The next day Trina went straight to Maggie.

Trina spoke in English. "You are welcome. That is the lesson for yesterday. And I am sorry. This is my lesson for today."

"All right, Trina," Maggie said. "Now you have to teach me how to say 'I'm sorry' too."

"So easy," said Trina. "*I am sorry. Lo siento.*"

Maggie repeated the words. "*Lo siento.*"

October came, and the boxcar was still in its place on the siding.

If only Papa could stay in this Wyoming town always. If only the engine would never hook on their boxcar and take them on to another place.

Now the pastures were dry and brown. The lame ewe still came to the fence, and Trina pulled grass for her to eat.

The leaves on the little trees near the hotel turned a brilliant yellow.

"It will soon be Halloween," Jaime said. "Pablo and Flavio and I are going out after dark and have fun."

"Mama," Trina said. "May I go with the boys and play tricks?"

"What do you mean, play tricks?" Mama asked.

"We don't want her," Jaime said.

"What does she mean, play tricks?" Mama asked Jaime.

"Oh, nothing much. Maybe we knock on a door and hide. Things like that." Jaime stood first on one foot and then on the other, and Trina knew that he wasn't telling everything.

"May I go, Mama?" Trina asked.

Papa spoke from his chair by the stove. "No. You may not. It is all right for boys to play their small, harmless tricks. Girls stay home."

"You can have a pumpkin lantern instead," Jaime said. "I'll help you make it."

Just before Halloween Jaime brought home a big pumpkin.

"Where did you get it?" Trina asked.

"Charlie Wilson's father got two in Cheyenne, and he gave one of them to me."

Their father sliced off the top, and Jaime and Trina scooped out the middle.

"The middle we will cook," Mama said. "Now."

With a pencil point, Jaime scratched two eyes and a nose and a laughing, toothy smile, and there was a pumpkin lantern with a fat, happy face.

"We need a candle to put inside," Jaime said.

"A little one," Trina said.

Mama opened the chest and lifted out her treasures. She set aside a small cardboard box and a cigar box.

"May I look in the cardboard box?" Trina asked.

It was a special treat to look in the cardboard box with its broken ends and its crumpled tissue paper. Trina knew what she would find there: a big gold heart that had been her mother's when her mother was a little girl. Trina loved the heart. She looked inside and lifted the heart. She put a fingernail in the small crescent at the side, and the heart swung open on small golden hinges. There was a picture inside.

It was funny and old-fashioned, but Trina loved it. There were three people in the picture: Grandfather and Grandmother in Mexico, young and different from the way Trina remembered them, with her mother, very small and smiling, standing at their knees.

Trina closed the locket and set it in its frame of tissue and put the lid on the box.

Mama lifted the cover of the cigar box. Inside were the ends of candles that had burned low. "I have exactly what you need," she said. "Here."

Jaime dug out a small place in the bottom of the pumpkin and set the candle inside.

"Now it's ready," Trina said.

After supper on Halloween, Jaime pulled on his heavy jacket.

"Don't stay out late," Mama said. "I do not like this custom of going out after dark and playing tricks on our neighbors."

"But we cannot take from this country only those things we like best," Papa said. "We will learn to enjoy all its customs."

Mama shook her head.

The pumpkin lantern was still burning when Jaime came back. He tossed his cap on a chair and wriggled out of his jacket.

"What did you do?" Trina asked. "Where did you go?"

"Oh, we knocked on the superintendent's window and scared Maggie and Mrs. Tolley. And we took Mr. Green's sign and hung it upside down."

"If Mr. Green comes here in the morning and asks that you replace it, right side up, I will not object," said Papa.

"Who went with you?" Trina asked.

"Flavio and Ricardo and Pablo, and Charlie Wilson, and the other boys."

"And what else did you do, Jaime?" Papa asked.

"Oh, we turned over the old bench on the hotel porch. But we didn't hurt it any. Just things like that."

It was obvious that Jaime wanted to change the subject. He was worried for fear Papa would ask too many questions, but Papa didn't.

"Time for bed," Mama said in English. "Blow out the pumpkin."

"Blow out the *candle*, you mean, Mama," Jaime said.

Trina took a long time getting ready for bed. She undressed Ana Maria and put her in the bunk in her petticoat. Then she got ready for bed herself and whispered her prayers.

Before breakfast the next morning, there was a loud knocking at the door. Trina's father slid it open.

Mr. Wilson was outside, and anyone could tell that he was very angry.

IO

"MR. GONZALES," Mr. Wilson said. "Last night some of the boys around town put my young bull in the hayloft, and I know that Jaime was with them. I want you and Jaime to come and help get it down."

"JAIME," Mr. Gonzales thundered. "DID YOU PUT THE BULL IN THE HAYLOFT?"

"No sir," Jaime said. His voice sounded small and squeaky. Like a scared mouse, Trina thought. "I didn't go near that . . ."

Mr. Wilson interrupted. "Jaime, were you with Pablo and Ricardo and the rest of those boys who

went around hanging signs upside down and turning over the hotel benches?"

"Yes sir, but . . ."

"I saw all of you going by the stables on the way
to the barn." Mr. Wilson was shouting.

"Charlie was with us," Jaime said. "Charlie will
tell you that we didn't even . . ."

"I know my Charlie was with that gang," Mr.
Wilson said. "I'm not excusing him. Charlie will
help get that bull down. Now I want you both to
come along with me. We've got to figure some way
to get that bull down before he hurts himself."

"We'll go," Jaime's father said. He gave Jaime
a push between the shoulder blades. "Go."

Mr. Wilson led the way, and Mr. Gonzales followed with a grip on Jaime's arm. Jaime hopped
along, one shoulder higher than the other.

Trina followed a distance behind them. She
hoped that her father would not turn around and
tell her to go home. She would like to see everything and hear everything that was said. Jaime was
in real trouble.

Mr. Marshall and Abner had already arrived.
Abner had his box camera and was taking a picture of the bull in the hayloft door. Mr. Green was

there too, and Charlie Wilson was kicking at the side of the barn.

The other fathers from the boxcars came with Pablo, Ricardo, and Flavio.

All the fathers were talking.

Mr. Green was on one knee beside a large coil of rope.

"As I see it," he said, "we have to make a harness strong enough to get that bull down." He looked at Mr. Wilson and nodded toward the door of the loft. "Is that pulley up there strong enough to hold a bull?"

"It's strong enough to hold this young bull," Mr. Wilson said. "What I'd like to know is how these boys got him up there." He turned to Charlie. "Did you use a rope and that pulley?"

Charlie shrugged his shoulders.

Mr. Green uncoiled the rope. "If we lay the rope like this — and tie it in place . . ."

They were weaving a harness — a place here for the bull's head, a place there for its legs, loose around the neck.

And then they were all going inside.

Papa suddenly became aware of Trina. "*Trina,* what are you doing here?"

"I want to see, Papa," Trina said. "I'll stay outside. I won't get in the way."

"Let her stay, Mr. Gonzales," said Mr. Wilson. "She can stay outside."

"Very well," Papa said. "Stand back out of the way."

Trina peeked through a crack between two boards.

They were all going up the big stairs that led steeply to the loft. Mr. Wilson was first.

There was scuffling and shouting in the loft, and Mr. Wilson's voice was louder than the rest.

"GOOD, WE'VE GOT HIM. EASY DOES IT. HANG ON. GET THE ROPE OVER THE PULLEY. HANG ON TIGHT. BRACE YOURSELF. SLIDE ALONG EASY. NOT SO FAST."

And the bull was coming down, suspended at the end of a rope, wound in its harness — slowly, slowly.

When it touched the ground, it scrambled about trying to free itself from the ropes. Mr. Wilson herded it into the barn.

All the fathers were tight-lipped.

Trina looked at the stern expression on her father's face. "He looks like a thundercloud," she thought. "There will be a big storm in our boxcar when we get home."

The parents and their sons started for home. Trina stayed to take one more look at the bull.

"*Espéranse,* wait," she said. "*Ven legerito,* come quick. *El toro,* the bull!"

The bull was climbing the stairs.

He disappeared into the hayloft.

Mr. Wilson scratched his ear. "Well, what do you think about that? He climbed those stairs by himself. You could knock me over with a feather."

"We will help you once more," Mr. Gonzales said. "We will help you get that bull down. Perhaps then you will be willing to tie him in his stall so this does not happen again?"

On their way home, Papa walked between Jaime and Trina. He put his hand on Jaime's shoulder.

Trina waited for Papa to speak.

II

"I HOPE you will excuse me," Papa said to Jaime. "Many times you will observe that parents are in the wrong." He nodded at Trina. "And you will also notice that mistakes are made as easily in English as in Spanish."

They walked on in silence. When they were crossing the tracks, Jaime spoke.

"Do you know what, Papa? Getting that bull out of the hayloft was more fun than Halloween."

Halloween was no sooner past than winter arrived. The ground was covered with snow. A white bedspread over the earth, Trina thought. When she walked against the wind, the cold hurt the bones of her face.

Shortly before Christmas, Mama decided that they would have a *piñata* on Christmas afternoon for the children of their town. This would be a Mexican party right in their own boxcar.

Jaime and Trina made the *piñata*.

Jaime covered one side of a big paper sack with crayon pictures. He drew a snorting bull, a fat pig, and a cactus plant with stickers.

Trina drew pictures on the other side of the sack. She drew a small brown bird, a little bare tree, and a gray-white ewe behind a barbed wire fence.

They fastened crepe-paper streamers to the bottom of the bag.

Their mother filled the bag almost to the top with hard candies from the store, and they fastened the *piñata* to the middle of the roof.

There it hung, bright in all the glorious colors of a box of crayons, and it was bulging with good things to eat.

If Trina walked under it, she could feel the streamers brushing her face. And when the door was opened, they flew around madly, like pennants in a great wind.

"You may ask your friends to come Christmas afternoon," Mama said.

"I'll invite them," Jaime said. "It takes Trina all day to say something."

"It doesn't either," Trina said. "I speak better all the time."

Jaime agreed. "You speak better. But slow, Trina."

When he came home, he threw his cap on a chair. "They are all coming," he said.

"Even the girls?" Trina asked.

"All of them," Jaime said.

On Christmas afternoon the boys came flashing down the hill on their sleds. They beat the snow from their clothes and stamped their feet before they went inside.

At two o'clock everyone had arrived, and the boxcar was full of boys and girls. Everyone was talking fast, and no one waited for Trina, and she didn't care.

She and Maggie stood side by side, and they were laughing together.

"It's time to break the *piñata*," Jaime said. "Everyone has to stand back, away from the stick. Trina will show how we swing the stick."

Their mother tied a blindfold over Trina's eyes and Jaime gave her a shove toward the center of the boxcar.

Trina swung her stick. There was screaming and laughing.

"Trina, you almost hit it," Charlie Wilson said.

"One more time," Jaime said. "Everybody gets two chances."

Trina tried. Her stick swished through the air. Again, she had missed.

Mama took off the blindfold. "Jaime will try." Mama was speaking in English! The blindfold was tied around Jaime's eyes.

"We go first," Jaime said, "because when the *piñata* breaks, the one who has the blindfold on doesn't get anything that falls out of the bag."

"No fair putting your head back and looking under," Charlie said. He gave Jaime a push.

Jaime held his stick as though it were a bat, and swung with all his might. It was a wild swing. He tried again.

"You'll never make a good baseball player," Flavio said. "Give me that stick."

With his blindfold tied on securely, Flavio missed twice.

Elizabeth hit the sack the first time she tried. The sack broke and candies flew everywhere. All the boys and girls were crawling over the linoleum, hunting. Trina divided hers with Elizabeth, who still had the blindfold over her eyes.

After they had eaten sweet rolls and drunk chocolate from little white paper cornucopias, the party was over.

"*Hasta la vista,* until we meet again," Mama was saying.

And all the boys and girls answered in Spanish — "*Hasta la vista.*"

All the rest of the afternoon the boys and girls walked up the hill and slid down. Trina sat behind Charlie Wilson on his long sled, and Maggie held on tightly behind her.

There was no need for words.

"Sometimes it's nice to have words and to speak them easily," Trina thought. "But sometimes it doesn't matter. Like now. There is a language that doesn't need words." She felt the tears on her cheeks. Happy tears. And the wind was cold, and she knew that she was happier than she had ever been before.

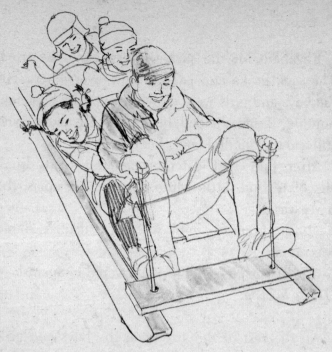

Trina ducked behind Charlie as they swerved down the hill, and it was a most magnificent day. *"Magnífico,"* thought Trina.

She knew that she would always remember this Christmas day.

Papa brought home a new calendar from the stables, and January had a picture of a beautiful white horse on a snow-covered hill. Trina marked off the days as they passed, and then one morning the west wind shifted to the east and the day grew cold and colder. News came over the telegraph at the railroad station that a storm was on the way.

"It's going to be a freeze," the man at the station said. "It will be the biggest freeze we've had in years."

"That means we'll have to get the sheep out of the state," Mr. Marshall said. "Order all the stock cars you can get. We'll round them up and ship them out."

In the distance the wagons of the sheepherders were gathered together, and the herders themselves were rounding up the bands of sheep and turning them toward the pens.

Beyond, the Big Horn Mountains were outlined in white against a gray sky.

All day the sheepherders worked. Dogs barked and men shouted. Freight trains rumbled into place and stood waiting, and the goat was brought down from the hotel to lead the sheep into the stock cars.

Warm, in two sweaters, a heavy coat, and a long purple stocking cap, Trina watched the loading. She watched for a long time.

"What happens if a sheep gets left behind?" she asked.

"One left behind would freeze solid," Pablo said.

"And that's the truth," Mr. Marshall said. "That's why we have to find every last sheep and get it shipped out of here. A sheep can stand a lot of cold, but it can't stand weather like this."

"But do you find every sheep?" Trina waited for the answer.

"We try," Mr. Marshall said.

12

TRAIN AFTER TRAIN pulled out, filled with sheep.

Trina looked for the tame ewe, even though she knew it would be almost impossible to see her among the hundreds of sheep that were being loaded into the cars.

Suddenly she knew that the ewe would not be here. She knew where she would find it.

She started down beside the tracks, running in the cinders. She followed the fence as fast as she could run — and there it was, where it always waited for her. It was waiting now.

Trina stepped on the lower strand of wire and held up the middle, and the ewe walked through.

Trina wound her fingers in its fleece, and they started toward the railroad station. The last train was moving out.

Trina saw the gray-white fleece of hundreds of sheep through the slats of the stock cars, and this one, this ewe, was left behind.

Trina took it straight to her own boxcar.

Mama took one look. "No," she said. "Impossible. You can see for yourself that we do not have room for the sheep. Go to the hotel. Perhaps they will shelter it with the goat."

"Mama's right," Jaime said. "Do what Mama says."

Trina found a short piece of rope and tied it around the ewe's neck.

"Silly sheep," Jaime said. "A sheep never knows which way to go. It has to follow something."

"It has me." Trina felt like kicking Jaime's shins, but she didn't.

She started off, leading the ewe. Then she saw a small figure coming down the hill. It was fat with clothes, and a blue stocking cap did not entirely cover the red hair. It was Maggie on her way to help. She started to run, arms outstretched to keep balanced.

"What happened? Did the sheep get left behind?"

"Sí. Yes," Trina said. "Mama said perhaps they will keep the ewe at the hotel."

"We've got an old chicken house. It's empty. It could stay there."

They tried once more to start the ewe up the hill.

"It's decided it won't follow," Maggie said. "Let's push."

The ewe refused to move.

Jaime came trudging up the hill through the snow. "Want me to get the goat? She'll follow the goat." He hurried on up the hill to the hotel.

Trina and Maggie stamped their feet to keep warm. Now and then the ewe bleated, as the snow settled thickly on its fleece.

And then Jaime was back, leading the goat, and the ewe followed the goat up the hill, past the hotel to Maggie's gate.

"Mama," Maggie said. "Is it all right if we put the ewe in the chicken house? They forgot her. And she'll freeze if we leave her outside."

"Of course it's all right," Mrs. Tolley said. "One of you go to the store and ask Mr. Green if he'll bring some feed over for her."

"I'll go," Jaime said.

Mr. Green came with feed and a bucket for water. The ewe ate, and steam rose up from its back.

Together the girls pushed the door shut and slid the bolt.

"There," said Maggie. "She's safe."

"I'll take the old goat back to the hotel," Jaime said. "And you'd better hurry home, Trina."

On the way home Trina thought about the people in her town: Maggie, Miss Grace, Mrs. Tolley, Mr. Green. This was *her* town, the best in Wyoming. And she was remembering English words. Little by little, *poco a poco*, she was remembering. She would forget that the engine might move their boxcar to another town. She shut her mind against the thought.

That night the wind howled, and it grew colder and colder. Trina's father kept the fire in the stove burning all the night through, and her mother piled coats and sweaters on their bunks. Far in the distance a coyote howled mournfully.

Trina shivered and huddled into a tight bundle between her blankets, and soon slept.

In the morning Papa said, "Go straight to school. Don't stop along the way. This is a morning when nose and ears may freeze quickly. Go."

"But the ewe," Trina said. "I was going to feed the ewe."

"I will feed her for you," Jaime said. "But when the big freeze is over, you will have to feed her yourself."

Trina thought this was fair. Remembering Papa's warning, she ran all the way to school.

The big black stove in the center of the schoolroom was glowing red, and everything was welcoming and warm. Miss Grace was writing arithmetic problems on the blackboard.

When Jaime arrived, the end of his nose was as white as chalk.

"Teacher," Trina said, "please look. Jaime's nose."

"Outside," Miss Grace said. "Quickly."

Trina stood in the doorway and watched while Miss Grace rubbed snow against Jaime's nose until it was pink.

"I couldn't feel it," Jaime said. "Now it prickles." All morning he wriggled his nose.

When the snow melted and the days were warmer, Trina and Maggie took the ewe back to the fence.

Maggie stepped on the bottom strand of the wire and propped up the middle strand. Trina stepped through and the ewe followed.

The stock cars rolled back to town, bringing a band of sheep to its own pasture, and the ewe followed them.

At school Trina had gone through the second reader once, and many more times at home.

"You are ready to read in the third reader," Miss Grace said. "We will start now."

Trina took the book home every night.

The weeks went by.

One evening Papa balanced the third reader in his big hand. "We have been through this book three times. We are ready to study the next."

"But that would be Jaime's book," Trina said.

"We will borrow it. Why should we let Jaime get ahead of us in reading this English?" asked Papa.

Trina opened the book to the first lesson in the fourth reader.

"Slower," said Papa. "You are reading too fast."

When there were only sixteen days to wait until Easter, Mr. Green received his shipment of Easter hats. Trina saw the box when it arrived. She ran downhill at top speed.

Trina huffed between her words. "Mr. — Green — has — the — Easter hats."

"This is important." Her mother took off her apron and tied the strings together. "I see no reason for waiting." She hung the apron on a nail. "Half the pleasure in the hat is looking at it before Easter."

When they opened the door at Mr. Green's store, he was unpacking the last of the hats.

"Mama, look."

The hats were the color of autumn fields, tawny tan, and each had a band of ribbon around the crown, with streamers hanging down the back.

"Try this one," Mr. Green said.

The hat came too far over Trina's forehead.

Mr. Green took the hat back and reached for another. He looked inside the crown. He reached for another. And another. "Funny. These seem to be the same size. I had Trina and Maggie in mind when I ordered. There ought to be two that are not so big." He looked through the entire stack. "Now isn't that too bad. What about putting a piece of cardboard inside the headband?"

Trina waited hopefully.

"I'll take one more look," Mr. Green said. He rummaged through the hats. "This might be smaller. Try this."

The hat had long black streamers. Her mother set it on Trina's head and slipped the elastic band under her chin. Trina looked over her shoulder. The streamers reached lower than her waist.

"Do you like it?" Trina's mother asked.

"*Me gusta*. I like it," Trina said.

Her mother laid two silver dollars on the counter, and Mr. Green punched the cash register four times. It clanged and a drawer flew open. He gave her mother fifteen cents in change.

Proudly Trina carried the big paper sack that held her new hat.

A covey of sage hens scurried across the roadway and hid in the brush near the pasture. The ewe came trotting across the field, bleating placidly.

Trina held the sack tightly.

This was a happy day.

She could hardly wait for Easter.

13

AND FINALLY EASTER ARRIVED — a beautiful day.

"Church will be at Mr. Wilson's house," Papa said. "We must be there at nine o'clock. And we must not be late."

"Sí, *Papá, entendemos*," Trina said.

"Yes, Papa, we understand," Jaime said.

"Good. If we understand in both Spanish and English, then surely we will be on time," Papa said.

Trina wore her best dress, white with a blue sash, and she set her hat on the top of her head. Its elastic band was tight under her chin. Proudly she walked up the hill. Her ribbon streamers whipped out in the wind.

On the Saturday after Easter, Trina and her mother were walking together on the way to the post office. Far to the left the little bands of sheep roamed together, and on the hill beside the hotel one little cross looked almost as though it had been etched against the sky.

"That little cross, Mama," Trina said. "Does it have something to do with Easter?"

"The cross marks a grave," Mama said. "When we first came here, Papa asked about it. He was told that long ago a little child was buried there."

"Who was the child?" Trina asked.

"No one knows," her mother said. "This is all I know, so this is all I can tell."

Trina felt sad to think of the child, dead so long ago, alone on the top of the hill.

She forgot about the cross until one unhappy morning when she was feeding the ewe at the side of the road. As she reached down for a handful of weeds, her fingers touched something dry and stiff. She parted the grasses and there was a bird lying on its back, its tiny claws twisted and tight.

Carefully she picked it up. It was cold and dead. She carried it home. "Look, Mama."

"A little sparrow," her mother said. "Do not look so sad. This is natural."

Jaime looked at the bird. "It's dead all right. Why don't we bury it? We can have a funeral."

Mama touched Trina's shoulder. "There is that wooden cigar box in the chest. Remember? You may have it to bury the bird in if you wish."

"I'll get one of Papa's spades," Jaime said.

"You may wrap the bird in a scrap of red calico," their mother said.

Trina held the bird in the palm of her hand. It was so light, so little, so dry.

Her mother opened the chest and reached for the cigar box. She emptied the candle ends into the chest and lined the box with a tiny piece of cloth. Trina laid the bird there and gently folded the cloth over it.

"I will carry the box," Jaime said.

"I will carry it," Trina said. "The bird is mine."

At the top of the hill they saw Charlie Wilson standing in front of the livery stable with his father.

"Hey, Charlie, come to our funeral," Jaime called.

"What are you burying?" Charlie asked.

Trina and Jaime answered at the same time.

"A poor little sparrow," Trina said.

"A dead bird," Jaime said.

Maggie came running down her walk. "What's in the box?"

Trina lifted the lid and waited to show her.

"We're going to have a funeral," Jaime said.

"Where will you bury it?" Maggie asked.

Trina looked up at the hill beside the hotel. "We will bury it there beside the big cross, where the little child lies."

"Gee, you're talking English," Jaime said. "Good."

"A long sentence," Charlie Wilson said. He looked at the bird. "We'll have to have a cross for it."

"But only a tiny one," Maggie said. "A bird-size cross."

Charlie's father was still leaning against the door of the stable. "Come on over," he said. "We can find a couple of scraps of wood somewhere."

It didn't take long to lay a short piece of wood over a longer and to drive in three small nails.

They started toward the big cross on the hill.

Five furry-looking prairie dogs watched curiously from their burrows. They popped out of sight as the procession passed: Trina and Maggie, Jaime and Charlie. Abner Marshall came hurrying to catch up with them.

Jaime dug a hole and set the box in it. He covered it over with sun-baked earth. When he had finished, they all patted the dirt until there was a tiny neat mound, and Charlie set the little cross in the ground.

"Now we can say a prayer," Trina said.

When the prayer was over, Trina brushed the dirt from her stockings.

"And we have to pick flowers," Maggie said.

"That's for girls," Jaime said. "Come on fellows, we're through."

Together Maggie and Trina hunted among the sparse weeds for the wild flowers that grew there — Johnny-jump-ups, buttercups. They laid them on the sparrow's grave.

Trina looked at the big cross. "There are flowers enough for two." She picked up half of them. Already their stems were growing limp. She laid them on the ground in front of the big cross.

From the top of the hill she could see in every

direction — down to the pasture, sagebrush green, over the roof of the hotel, to the town with its brown buildings, to their own boxcar and the gray-blue sky that covered everything.

"For the bird this is almost as good as a treetop," she thought, "and the little child is not alone."

Afterward she and Maggie got their dolls and took them to the fence to see the lame ewe. Maggie held her own doll and Ana Maria as well, while Trina gathered wild oats for the ewe. The ewe looked almost like the picture on the calendar at home for the month of May. Perhaps this ewe wasn't quite as white, but she was trusting and friendly.

On the May month on the calendar, Trina had circled one special day. And one morning the day finally came. Trina awakened early and knew that this was a special and wonderful time.

14

"H<small>APPY</small> <small>BIRTHDAY</small>," Papa said. He was standing in his nightshirt and his hair was tousled. He turned to Mama. "And do we not have a present for her from the chest?"

"Perhaps we should wait until we are dressed and have had breakfast?" Mama was smiling, almost as though she knew what the answer would be.

"No, no, please, Mama," Trina said.

"Now," Papa said.

"After breakfast," Jaime said.

Mama lifted the lid of the chest and removed the small cardboard box.

"Mama," Trina said. "Not the locket?"

"The locket," Mama said quietly. She opened the box and held up a long chain with a big gold heart on it. She slipped it over Trina's head. It hung low on her nightgown. "As my mother gave it to me long ago, so now it goes to you, with love from Papa and me."

Trina hugged and kissed her mother and father.

Jaime lifted the chain with his forefinger and thumb. "It's too long for you. It hangs almost to the waist. The heart is too big. It doesn't look American."

Trina kicked his shin.

"Ow," Jaime said. "Ow-ow. Did you see what she did, Mama?"

"Careful," Mama said. "One more kick and we will forget who has the birthday."

While she was dressing, Trina worried about the size of the heart. Jaime was wrong. Surely he was wrong. It wasn't too big. She loved it.

Breakfast was special — eggs and fried beans, sweet rolls, and a mug of steaming coffee. She sipped the coffee even though she didn't like the taste.

First the locket and now coffee. Trina felt entirely grown up.

This birthday was also special because it was Saturday, and this meant that after breakfast she would go up the hill to Maggie's house.

On the way up the hill, she was looking at her locket and almost bumped into Charlie Wilson, who was on the way down.

"What have you got?" Charlie asked.

Trina opened her hand wide. "It's my birthday present."

"Gee, that's the biggest heart I ever saw."

She closed her fingers over the locket. It was not too big. It was just right. She hated boys. She went up the hill to Maggie's house.

Maggie was on the front steps with her doll when Trina arrived. Her doll wore the flower-sprigged dress.

"Look at my birthday present," Trina said. "Maybe the heart is too big?"

Maggie looked at the locket. "No, it isn't too big," she said. "It's just right. It's the kind you can grow into. You can wear it forever."

On the way home Trina walked slowly, swinging the heart on the end of the chain, which felt heavy and good around her neck.

Away across the sagebrush flat, groups of prong-horns[1] ran swiftly, their white tails flashing in the sunshine.

At the railroad station Trina saw the big pig rooting around a rubbish can. Trina let the heart hang free — for the pig wore a hat! A hat with black ribbons.

"*¡Pare! Mi sombrero!* My hat," Trina shouted. "Stop. *Pronto.*"

She started after the pig, and he grunted and trotted up the hill.

"*Mi sombrero,*" Trina shouted again.

Charlie Wilson came galloping down the hill with Abner Marshall, zigzagging across to block the pig's progress.

"You're talking Spanish!" Abner yelled. "THAT PIG DOESN'T UNDERSTAND SPANISH."

Trina reached for the pig's tail. It slipped through her fingers, and she stumbled and fell.

"It's an *English* pig," Charlie Wilson said. "If you want your hat, ask him politely in *English.*"

[1] wild antelope

"I will ask with a stick," Trina said, as she picked herself up.

The boys fell against each other laughing.

Trina's hat had slipped to one side, and the pig stood with his front feet apart and regarded them suspiciously.

Abner grabbed the pig around the middle and Charlie slipped the elastic chin-band from its head. Trina grabbed the hat and ran. Charlie and Abner were shouting with laughter.

Trina started shouting for her mother before she reached the boxcar.

"Mama, *mi sombrero*. My hat. Jaime put it on the pig. *Mi sombrero*."

The hat was crumpled, and the streamers had dragged in the dirt. Mama stood in the car door.

"Jaime did it." Trina's voice sounded small, and she knew she would cry.

"Never mind," Mama said. "Let me see the hat. When Jaime comes home, we will speak with him. As for the hat, I will brush it and I will iron the brim."

"But the ribbons, Mama?"

"We will cut off the ends of the ribbons and you will not know that the pig has worn the hat."

"But Charlie and Abner will know, Mama. Every time they see me wear my hat, they'll remember."

"The world has not ended," Mama said. "You still have the hat. Call Jaime, please, and tell him that I wish to talk with him."

Trina was glad to call Jaime, who did not come. He did not come until suppertime.

Papa heard the story and he talked to Jaime.

"On Monday, after school, you will let the pig wear your Sunday cap. Then you will know how Trina feels about her hat."

Trina could hardly wait until Monday.

15

On Monday, after school, Trina reminded Jaime about his cap. "Papa said. Remember what Papa said?"

"And I have one question to ask," Mama said. Jaime traced a linoleum rose with his toe.

"Why did you put Trina's hat on the pig?" Mama asked.

"I don't know," Jaime said. "When I did it, it seemed like a good idea."

Mama thought about this. "Anyone can make a mistake. Perhaps when you have another idea, it will be well to think twice."

Jaime got his Sunday cap and hopped down out of the boxcar. Trina followed. This would be wonderful.

Charlie and Flavio Valdez helped Jaime fasten strings to the buttons on the side of his cap. Charlie got his father's red and white striped necktie and tied it around the pig's head. Abner Marshall was there with his box camera.

The pig walked along Main Street wearing Jaime's cap and Mr. Wilson's necktie.

A lot of people came to look and to laugh. Mrs. Tolley and Mrs. Green, Mrs. Marshall and Maggie.

Mr. Wilson came out of his livery stable and laughed louder than anyone, until he saw that the necktie was his.

Abner Marshall took three different pictures, because the first time he forgot to wind the film.

Maggie and Trina stood together.

Mr. Wilson was calling for Charlie, but Charlie had disappeared, and everyone stopped laughing.

Abner and Jaime caught the pig and took off the cap and the tie.

At home Trina dusted off Jaime's cap. She was glad that it looked much the same as it had before. Perhaps one of the buttons was a little bit loose.

She looked at the calendar. June. The picture showed a flock of sheep in a meadow dotted with daisies. June was circled, too, for the last day of school.

When the last week of school came, Miss Grace looked very proud.

"You have done well. All of you. Pablo, Ricardo, Charlie, Jaime, Maggie, everyone. And you, Trina, I'd like to see what you can do with the fourth reader. I have the idea that you have done better than I have realized."

Trina smiled to herself. Many times she and her father had been through this book at home.

She read from the reader.

"Trina, Trina. This is wonderful," said Miss Grace. "You are a lucky girl. And Jaime is lucky, and Pablo and Ricardo and Flavio. You are bilingual. You have two languages: English and Spanish. I am so glad that I will be coming back to this school next year."

All afternoon Trina thought about what had happened.

When Papa came home that night she told him the news.

"Papa, I have two languages: English and Spanish. Thank you, Papa, for helping me."

"You are welcome." Papa sounded sad. His voice was level and low. "You are welcome, Trina."

"Papa," Mama said, "*¿Que le pasa?* What is the matter?"

Papa glanced significantly at Trina. "I will tell you later, Mama. Now, let's enjoy Trina's success."

That night Trina sat in her bunk, swinging her gold heart on the end of its chain.

Clearly she heard Papa say to Mama, "The superintendent wants to see me in the morning. You know what this means, Mama."

Mama was silent.

Papa spoke again. "It means we will move on, Mama. Undoubtedly he will tell me that we are to go to another town. I am sad for all of us. This town is a good town. I am sad most of all for Trina."

Trina lay down with her cheek against the cool gold of the big heart. The tears rolled down her face and dampened her pillow.

16

THE NEXT MORNING Trina sat in the rocking chair and rocked slowly.

Before he went to work, Papa kissed her cheek loudly, but still Trina sat there.

"What is the matter?" Mama said. "Why are you so quiet? Good things have happened to you in school."

"I heard Papa," Trina said. "I don't want to leave this town. I don't want to move away. Maggie's here, and Teacher is coming back next year. She said so."

Mama touched her shoulder. "Do not make Papa sad when he comes home."

Trina swung the heart on its chain. She put her fingernail against the little crescent at the side of the heart, and the lid opened on its tiny hinges. There, on the left side, was a new picture. A big picture of a pig wearing a cap.

"Mama," Trina said. "*Look*. Jaime did this."

"Jaime," Mama said.

Jaime came from his bunk. "That's only a joke," he said. "Trina can't take a joke. Abner gave me the snapshot for a joke. He had four films left in his camera after he took that picture of the bull, and he took three of the pig — and this one. Here. Give me the locket." He removed the picture of the pig and replaced it with another.

"Mama, he's putting something else in. Make him give me my locket."

Jaime set the picture in the heart and pushed it around with his thumbnail. He handed it back to Trina. "There. Now you have all of us. You have the old picture of Grandmother and Grandfather and Mama on one side, and you have the new one with Papa and me on the other."

Mama looked over Trina's shoulder. "That is nice.

Very nice. You and Papa are smiling. Nice. But Trina is not there."

"I can always look in the mirror to see myself," Trina said. "Thank you, Jaime. I am sorry I kicked you."

"That's okay," Jaime said. "I had forgotten."

Trina carefully closed the heart. As Maggie had said, it was a locket to wear forever.

That night Papa came home. He tapped his chest with a forefinger. "If you please, look at me. Do I look like a man who brings bad news?"

"No," Mama said. "You bring good news. What has happened?"

"Sit down. Sit down and listen," Papa said. "I will tell you the whole story. Today, feeling very sad, I went to see the superintendent. The superintendent told me that more men are coming to work for the railroad. He talked with Ricardo's father and with Flavio's father and with me.

"He told us we were fine workmen — none better. This we knew," said Papa, "for we work hard. He needed one foreman. He handed a paper to Ricardo's father and asked him to read it. Ricardo's father said, 'I read only in Spanish.'

"The superintendent handed the paper to Flavio's father. The same thing. Then the superintendent handed the paper to me. 'I also read only in Spanish,' I said. Then I happened to look at the paper and I knew all the words. I read them all. I read them as well as *you* can read, Trina. And so I am the new foreman. I have this new job. This is America, where a man may go to the top if he will speak and read English."

Mama threw her arms around Papa's neck and was so excited that she spoke in Spanish.

Trina was not excited.

Of course this was nice for Papa and Mama. They were pleased. But always when Papa had a new job, the engine backed into the siding and hooked onto the boxcar, and the wheels started to roll again.

"Oh, Papa. I almost wish we hadn't read the books together."

"*¿Por qué?* Why?" asked Papa.

"I don't want to move away. I like it here."

"And who said we are to move away? A foreman stays here on the job. We do not move. Another thing, I will borrow the readers, for it is agreed that I shall teach Ricardo's father and Flavio's also. When more men come to work for the railroad, the

superintendent will need more foremen. They will
be ready."

"Will we live right here in our boxcar?" Jaime
asked.

"Certainly," said Papa. "Where else?"

"Wahoo," said Jaime. "WAHOO!"

The next day Miss Grace waited at the railroad
station for the train back to Denver. When the train
puffed in, all the boys and girls were there — sixteen of them.

The conductor helped Miss Grace aboard, and she stood on the back platform. He called "All aboard!" and then the train wheels slowly turned.

"Good-bye, Teacher, good-bye!"

"*Hasta la vista*," Miss Grace answered.

"Until next year, Teacher," Jaime called.

The boys and girls ran behind the train.

Faster and faster the wheels turned, and then finally the train was gone.

Jaime and the boys were marching, their arms

across each other's shoulders, laughing, keeping step.

Trina thought of the trains that would come and go, passing her own boxcar, here on the railroad siding, in her own most wonderful town.

The lame ewe stood waiting at the fence.

Maggie and Trina saw it, and both started talking at the same time, and then they stopped to laugh. There was so much to talk about, so many things to tell — and there was time for the telling.

GLOSSARY

a donde vas	*ah DOAN-deh vahs*	where are you going?
ahora	*ah-OR-a*	at once; now
anda, anda	*AHN-dah, AHN-dah*	go, go; "gitty up"
bien, y tu debiera llevar los paquetes. Estás andando a bicicleta	*be-EHN e too deh-be-ERA yeh-VAHR los pah-KEH-tes; ehs-TAHS ahn-DAHN-do ah bee-see-CLEH-tah*	good, and you should carry the packages; you're riding the bicycle
buenos días	*BWEHN-os DEE-uhs*	good morning
descansa; vuelvo pronto	*dehs-CAHN-sa VWEL-vo PRON-to*	rest; I will return soon

el toro	*el TOHR-ro*	the bull
en seguida	*ehn se-GUEE-dah*	at once, quickly
espéranse	*es-PEHR-an-se*	wait!
estás tan linda	*ehs-TAS tahn LEEN-dah*	you are so beautiful
este es mi pueblo y yo quiero quedarme acquí	*EHS-te ehs me poo-EHB-lo e yo kee-EHR-o keh-DAR-me ah-KEE*	this is my town and I want to stay here
este Jaime	*EHS-te HY-me*	that James!
hasta la vista	*AHS-ta lah VEES-ta*	until I see you
lo siento	*lo see-EHN-to*	I am sorry
magnífico	*mahg-NEE-fe-co*	magnificent
me gusta	*may GOOS-tah*	I like it
me llamo Trina	*may YAH-mo TREEN-ah*	My name is Trina
mi sombrero	*me som-BREH-ro*	my hat
mira, ve que ha pasado	*ME-rah, veh kay ah pah-SAH-do*	look! see what happened
nadie le esperaría	*NAHD-ia lay es-pehr-ar-REE-ah*	no one would wait for her
no me importa	*no meh eem-POR-tah*	I don't care
no, muy tarde	*no, MOO-ey TAHR-day*	no, too late
no tengo tiempo para cerdos hoy día	*no TEHN-go te-EHM-po PAH-ra SEHR-dos OI DEE-a*	I do not have time for pigs today

no voy a tu fiesta	*no voy ah too fee-EHS-ta*	I will not come to your party
nunca tan felíz	*NOON-cah tahn feh-LEEZ*	never so happy
pare	*PAH-ry*	stop!
piñata	*peen-YAH-tah*	A decorated container for small gifts
poco a poco	*po-co ah po-co*	little by little
por qué	*poar KEH*	why?
pronto	*PROAN-to*	quickly
que le pasa	*kay lay PAH-sa*	what is the matter?
ríense	*REE-ehn-see*	laugh
señor	*sen-YOR*	mister or sir
sí	*see*	yes
sí, Papá, entendemos	*see, pa-PAH ehn-tehn-DEH-mos*	yes, Papa, we understand
ven legerito	*vehn lay-gayr-REE-to*	come quickly
ven, ven	*vehn, vehn*	come, come
vete	*VEH-ty*	go away